5114

Please check all items for damages
before leaving the Library.
Thereafter you will be held
responsible for all injuries
to items beyond reasonable wear.

Helen M. Plum Memorial Library

Lombard, Illinois

A daily fine will be charged for
overdue materials.

JUN   2013

I FEEL HAPPY

By Katie Kawa

Gareth Stevens
Publishing

Please visit our website, www.garethstevens.com. For a free color catalog of all our high-quality books, call toll free 1-800-542-2595 or fax 1-877-542-2596.

Library of Congress Cataloging-in-Publication Data

Library of Congress Cataloging-in-Publication Data

Kawa, Katie.
 I feel happy / Katie Kawa.
     p. cm. — (How do I feel?)
 Includes index.
 ISBN 978-1-4339-8108-1 (pbk.)
 ISBN 978-1-4339-8109-8 (6-pack)
 ISBN 978-1-4339-8107-4 (library binding)
 1. Happiness in children—Juvenile literature. I. Title.
 BF723.H37K393 2013
 152.4'2—dc23
                                    2012020648

First Edition

Published in 2013 by
Gareth Stevens Publishing
111 East 14th Street, Suite 349
New York, NY 10003

Copyright © 2013 Gareth Stevens Publishing

Editor: Katie Kawa
Designer: Mickey Harmon

Printed in the United States of America

CPSIA compliance information: Batch #CW13GS: For further information contact Gareth Stevens, New York, New York at 1-800-542-2595.

Contents

My Birthday! 4

Fun with Friends. 10

A New Bike 16

Words to Know 24

Index. 24

Today is my birthday!
This makes me feel happy.

5

I am having a party with my friends.

My friends go
to my school.
I have eight friends
at my party.

9

Playing with my friends makes me happy.

11

We play with my dog.
His name is Max.

13

Then, we eat pizza
for dinner.

15

I get a new bike
for my birthday!
It is from my grandma.

17

I wear a helmet
when I go on my bike.
It keeps my head safe.

19

I ride my bike
to the park.
I go there with my dad.

21

I feel happy
when I ride my bike.
It makes me smile!

23

Words to Know

bike

friends

helmet

Index

bike 16, 18, 20, 22   friends 6, 8, 10

birthday 4, 16   party 6, 8